POPPY PICKLE

DISCLAIMER

NO CATS, DADS, FLYING PIGS, Woolly Mammoths, PET CROCODILES OR GIANT Talking HOT DOGS WERE HARMed in THE making OF THIS BOOK.

- - - - - - - -

This is a story about a little girl.

A very special little girl…

and her name is…

POPPY

A Templar Book

First published in the UK in 2015 by Templar Publishing,
part of the Bonnier Publishing Group,
Deepdene Lodge, Deepdene Avenue, Dorking, Surrey, RH5 4AT, UK
www.templarco.co.uk

Copyright © 2015 by Emma Yarlett

First edition

ISBN 978-1-78370-175-9 Hardback
ISBN 978-1-78370-176-6 Paperback

Edited by Alison Ritchie

Printed in China

templar publishing

PICKLE

Poppy Pickle lived in an ordinary house with an ordinary dad, an ordinary mum and three ordinary cats…

But Poppy Pickle was not ordinary. Far from it.

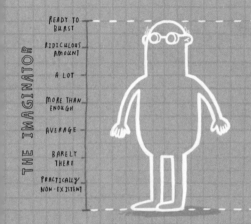

You see, Poppy Pickle was full to the brim with imagination.

Sometimes Poppy's imagination got her into a bit of a pickle.

Poppy went upstairs,
but she didn't tidy her room.

Instead
she started
imagining…

And suddenly the strangest
thing happened.

POP!

Her imagination came…

ALIVE!

It was incredible.
It was amazing.
It was **magic**.

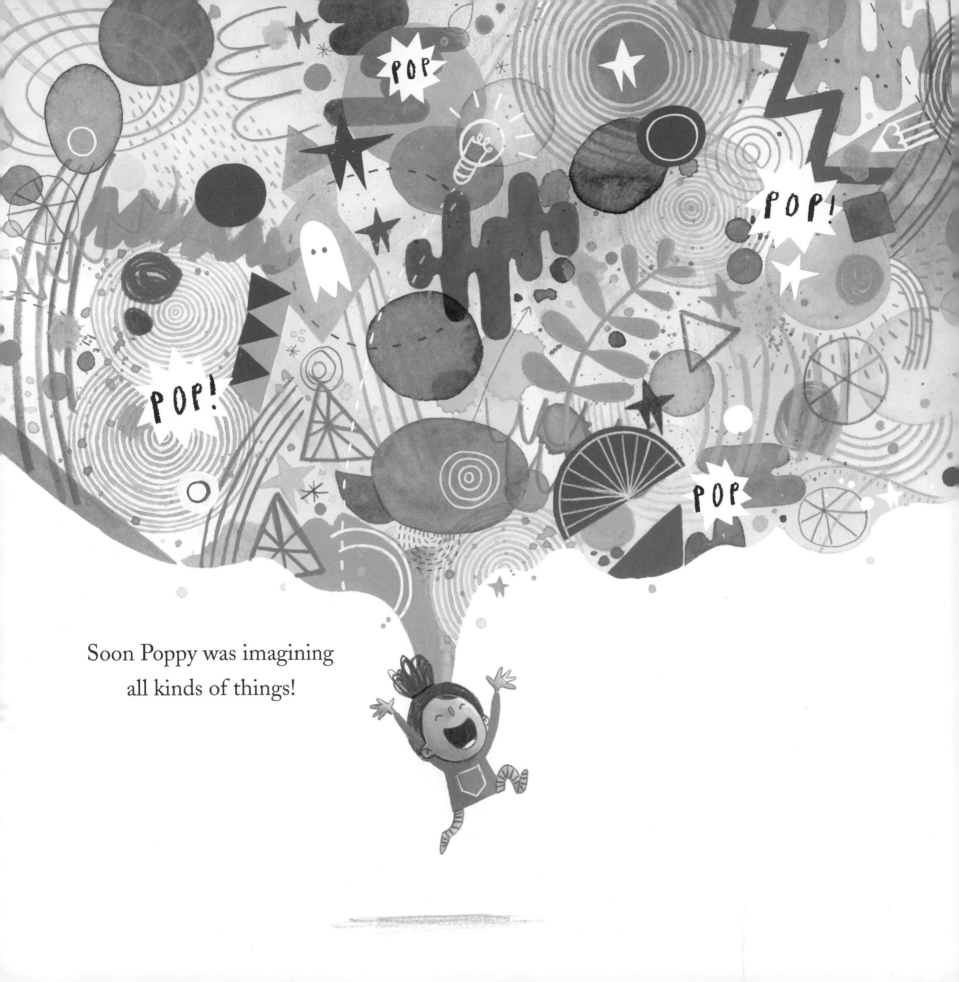

Soon Poppy was imagining
all kinds of things!

Poppy
imagined
big.

Poppy imagined small.

Poppy imagined far and inbetween and back to front and upside down.

Poppy Pickle imagined it **all**.

Soon Poppy's room was filled with
weird and wonderful creatures.

Poppy was having the time of her life.
Until...

...it all started to go **very,**

very

wrong.

And then everything went
from very wrong to
totally terrible!

Poppy was in a
huge pickle!

She had to get rid of everything FAST – before Mum and Dad found out!

Un-imagining the creatures didn't work... at... all!

So Poppy imagined
a giant eraser to rub
them out. But imaginary
creatures are very tricky
to catch, and Poppy was
running out of time.
Mum and Dad were
at the door.

Quick as a flash,
a **door** appeared.

It was hard work pushing everyone through…

But Poppy did it.

Just in time…

It took Poppy **all** afternoon to clear up the mess.
When she had finally finished it was dinner time…

and she was still in trouble.

Big trouble.

pop!